Snowball
the Sherlock Rabbit and the
Case of the Missing Fur

By Constance Meccarello-Gerson
Illustrated by Lucía Benito

Dedication

To my mother Angelina Meccarello who taught third grade for thirty years. I know if you were still with us, you would love Snowball.

Hi, I'm Snowball the Rabbit and one morning I woke up in my cozy warm rabbit den without my fur! But I wasn't alone. I went next door to the newlyweds Tommy and Sunny rabbit, my neighbors. They are a nice couple. Tommy is a long-haired male rabbit with lots of fur. It is a beautiful white and brown color. It was all gone. Sunny his wife was a young six-month-old rabbit with beautiful white fur. She was carrying their three-month baby Horace in a blue blanket. He blinked at me and smiled. Sunny had lost half her fur and the rest of her fur was suddenly grey from shock. She couldn't stop crying. Grey fur didn't look good on her either.

"Whatever happened," she sobbed, "at least they didn't take Horace's baby hair. " she showed me Horace minus the blanket, and he had fine brown baby rabbit fur all over.

"Thank goodness for that." I replied.

That said, I went home and put on my Sherlock Rabbit Cape and picked up my magnifying glass and went back next door.

Tommy and I had a talk. He offered to pay me twenty carrots if I found the rabbit who clipped us. It had to be another rabbit. No human would just take our fur. Humans would kill us for the pot. I agreed to the carrot payment for two reasons, I loved carrots and Tommy grew the best in the whole of the Rabbit Kingdom.

I went on the hunt! Maybe hunt is the wrong word for a furless rabbit to use. Anyway, I hopped over to the other three dens, Robert the Bunny home, George the Bunny home, and Nancy the Bunny home, in our neighborhood and every rabbit in those dens were the same, furless. No den had extra hair lying around so they were taken off my list of suspects. Lucky them! I hopped on.

There was a beautiful sparkling stream that was close enough for the local rabbits to hop to. I went to check there. It was a beautiful morning; the weather was nice. If it had been raining, without fur, I would have been cold. I looked around the shore, no fur there. Sitting on a green bank near the water was a pair of pink child's scissors. A very small pair, with pink handles. Near the scissors was a small hedgehog, he blinked at me. "Which way did the criminal go?" I asked.

In a soft hedgehog voice, he said, " A big rabbit hopped toward the great lawn."

So, I was looking for a very big rabbit, there were a few in the neighborhood who could handle child's scissors. From the color of the scissors, I may be looking for a female rabbit, they liked pink. If a female rabbit, she had to be big to handle those scissors. Why did female rabbits like pink? I didn't know.

A clue already and Sherlock Rabbit, me, was getting very excited. I had to leave the scissors; they were too heavy for me to drag back to my den. But I was on the right trail.

I hopped and hopped. Suddenly ahead on the smooth lawn of some human was a huge pile of bunny fur! All different colors of fur were sitting there. And as if on guard sat Slimey Rabbit. He was a huge bunny .Slimey didn't like me. He didn't like all my bunny neighbors. Slimey dated Sunny before she married Tommy. He is, as his name suggests, Slimey. He stole from other bunnies and kicked them with his big hairy feet if they followed him to get their carrots back. But with his dating Sunny, he wanted more than carrots.

So, we all in the neighborhood banded together in a Rabbit Seminar to figure out how to talk Sunny, the sweetest rabbit in the world, out of marrying Slimey. And why she needed to stop accepting his stolen carrots. And then, in the middle of our discussion, Tommy came up with a creative idea.

"Do you think she would marry me?" he asked.

Tommy was a wonderful handsome rabbit. He was young and gifted too. In his backyard he grew the most delicious carrots in town. What girl rabbit could refuse him? We set up a blind bunny date for both, with wonderous lettuce and Tommy's carrots to eat. They fell in love and were married a week later.

All the rabbits in the colony were very happy except one, Slimey, the big footed evil rabbit. Sunny even went to him, before the wedding and said she didn't really love him, just the carrots he gave her. Sad but true. He cursed Sunny and Tommy both in the church and promised rabbit revenge on them. And here he was taking it!

When he saw me as Sherlock Rabbit he started to laugh. I guess it was the cape or my small size. Perhaps due to my size he thought I could be defeated easily? Sherlock Rabbit had a surprise in his cloak for Slimey! I had a small spray bottle of homemade Rabbit Destroy Spray in my pocket. This spray I made of stink weed and alder tree. It was a secret recipe I had learned from my parents. Any normal or big rabbit would drop in a faint if sprayed by it. I sprayed Slimey rabbit. He was still laughing...

Then he blinked. And the next thing I knew is he fell over. It worked! Thank goodness it worked or I would have been in trouble.

Carefully, I walked up to him. He wasn't moving. In fact, he wasn't breathing. I dropped to the ground and gave him Rabbit CPR. He started to breathe! I was glad. I stood there over his big rabbit body. I hadn't meant to hurt him so badly. Then I whistled loudly. Rabbits came from everywhere all without fur to my call. We stood in a circle

We all sang the Rabbit Unhappy Song softly so humans couldn't hear us.

You are bad.

You are hairy.

You loved carrots and lettuce.

(and Me!) sang Sunny

You weren't kind.

You cut our hair.

We forgive you.

And so, the song went. As we sang each rabbit took his fur from the pile. We all walked slowly toward home. Slimey woke up during the song and started to cry.

"I'm sorry," he cried, "but I really loved Sunny. I understand now that she didn't really love me."

And turning our backs we, all walked humming, back home.

That night, Tommy knocked and delivered his beautiful carrots. We sat in my cozy den.

"Do you think my hair will ever grow back?" He asked as we both eat carrots.

"I hope so." I answered.

The End

This is the end of my Sherlock Rabbit Case. Tomorrow I would start The Case of The Missing Carrot Garden.

Stay tuned.

The History of Snowball, the Sherlock Rabbit

Snowball, the Rabbit was an excellent solver of puzzles and word games in school. His teacher Mrs. Paw, an old wise rabbit scholar, said to him one day, "Why you remind me of Sherlock Holmes the human detective who always solves crime."

So, Snowball added Sherlock to his rabbit name and started to solve rabbit crimes.

Where did real rabbits come from?

The first rabbits came from southern Europe. They evolved over millions of years. Ancient merchants referred to this part of the world as "I-sephan-im" which means Land of The Rabbits.

Constance Meccarello-Gerson was born in Poughkeepsie N.Y. She is a graduate of Florida Southern College with a BA in Acting. She also attended the American Academy of Dramatic Arts. HB Studio, Actors Studio, in NYC. She is a member of SAG, Alpha Gamma Delta, Alpha Si Omega. Her MFA in Acting is from Brooklyn College.

She has appeared on TV, film, and on stage in NYC. For 20 years she taught as a mentor and teacher of English and Theatre arts for the New York City Department of Education and for the University at Santa Cruz. She also taught for ten years as a Speech Coordinator at Touro College. She was an executive at Bloomingdales. Her writing as appeared in Reflections, also in the Best American Poets series. Currently she lives in NYC with her husband Alain, a parrot named Benji, and lots of fish.

Printed in Great Britain
by Amazon

83058361R00016